MISS MOLLY'S SCHOOL OF MAKING FRIENDS

Laura Cowan

Illustrated by Rosie Reeve

Designed by Tabitha Blore & Eleanor Stevenson

Edited by Anna Milbourne

Design Manager: Nicola Butler Digital manipulation: John Russell

First published in 2023 by Usborne Publishing Ltd., Usborne House, 83-85 Saffron Hill, London EC1N 8RT, England
usborne.com
First published in America in 2023. UE.

This is **Kerry**.

The idea of making new friends turns
her tummy upside down.

When she was little, Kerry already knew everyone who lived nearby.

And all the little animals who lived nearby went to her playgroup.

But the Koalas have just moved to a new house, and Kerry doesn't know **anyone** on her new street.

And she won't know anyone at her new school either. She feels very **small** and **scared**.

At the park, Kerry didn't want to go and play.

Her voice felt too **tiny** even to say hello.

But Kerry didn't want a hug.
She climbed as **fast** as she could all the way up the tree until...
Hello, Koalas. My name is Miss Molly. I wondered when you'd find me.

At the top of the tree was a school,
but not an ordinary school at all.
It was a school for **making friends**.

It was **just** what Kerry needed!

Friendship workshop
Thanks for listening.
A good friend ALWAYS listens.
It's your turn to choose a game!
Yay! Thank you.
Play library
Getting along studio
I'm sorry for shouting - I got angry.
That's OK. Thanks for apologizing.

"Hello, I'm Mrs. Hamster," said Kerry's first teacher. "The first step to making a new friend is saying hello. So, we're going to play a little game to try it out. When you catch the ball, say '**hi**', then throw it to someone else."

Hi!

Mrs. Hamster threw the ball to Kerry first...

Then Kerry threw the ball to a porcupine.

They both giggled. This was **fun**!

Next, the animals tried adding their names.

They tried adding a question, too. It all worked well until...

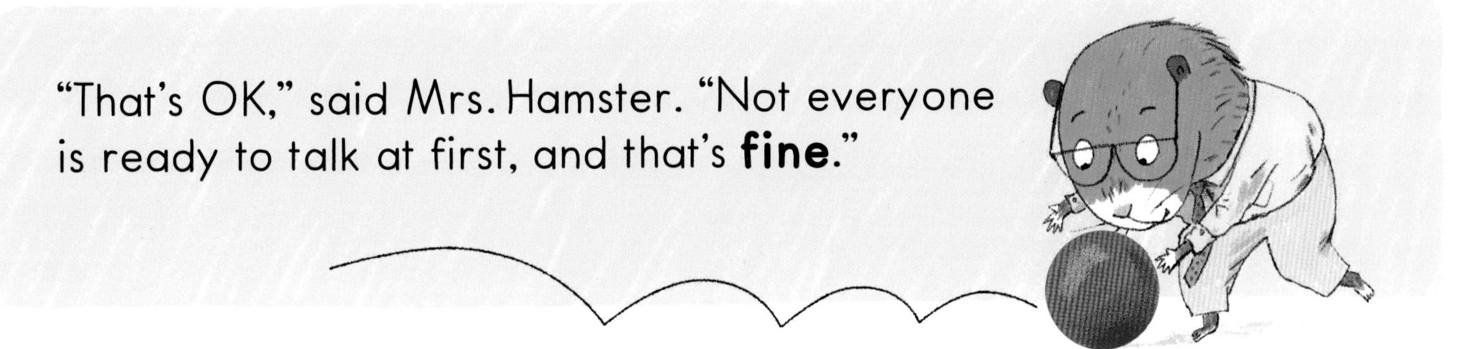

“That's OK,” said Mrs. Hamster. “Not everyone is ready to talk at first, and that's **fine**.”

Mrs. Hamster and Kerry tried to make Perry feel better.

Perry peeped his head out **very slowly** and gave Kerry a little smile.

Mrs. Hamster had another game to help with talking to new animals.

The animals got busy rolling cubes and asking each other the questions on them.
Do you have any pets?
I have a pet snail.
What do you like doing after school?
Playing in the woods!
What games do you like to play?
Board games!
Who's in your family?
Um... There's me, Grandma and Papa.
Next time you can't think of anything to say, try remembering one of these questions.
I will!

Some of the class needed help right away...

"When you can't decide who goes first in a game, try this rhyme," Mr. Tanuki said.

"Say the rhyme, pointing to the next animal as you say each word.

On the last word, whoever you're pointing to is the one who goes **first**!"

Mr. Tanuki asked the class to think of **fun** things to do with friends even when you don't have any toys.

They had lots of ideas...

Then the wombat twins started squabbling.

The twins didn't want to play the same thing **at all**.

Mr. Tanuki explained that they didn't have to. Friends might want to play alone sometimes, but it doesn't mean they're not your friend. If that happens, you can always ask someone **else** to play...

Kerry and Patty were also in a grump. Mr. Tanuki came over to help.

"Are you two OK?" he asked.

Mr. Tanuki had an idea to help everyone learn how to be a **good sport** whether they win or lose...

At the end of the game, everyone had to say something nice to someone on the other team. They could give a compliment, or say thank you or something comforting to someone who didn't win.

The class felt proud of themselves as they left for lunch.

After a treetop picnic, it was time for Ms. Chameleon's **getting along** class. Kindness helps everyone get along. So first of all, she asked them to think about the kind things their friends had done for them.

It's important to be kind to your friends, because it shows you care. So the class thought about all the kind things **they** had done for their friends, too.

"Being kind isn't always easy," said Ms. Chameleon. "Can you think of any times when you find it **hard** to be kind?"

It was for those times that Ms. Chameleon showed them how to be a good friend to themselves.

Just then Kerry's tummy **r-r-rumbled**, and everyone giggled.

"Now, let me show you my **sorry board**," said Ms. Chameleon.

"If you are ever unkind to your friends, you need to say sorry. Then your friends will know that you didn't want to upset them."

"But what if someone has been unkind to me, and didn't say sorry. What should I do?" Bim whispered.

"Even the best of friends don't get along **all** the time, Bim," Ms. Chameleon replied. "If your friends upset you, you may need to be very **brave** and let them know."

Bim tried this with Hannah...

But Hannah looked miserable.

"Good work, Bim," Ms. Chameleon said, "I know you were afraid to talk about how you felt, but being open and honest with a friend will only make your friendship **stronger**."

The final class of the day was with Miss Molly herself. Everyone gathered around the school **friendship bracelet**.

Each thread was a different shade and stood for a different part of friendship – the things friends like, what they enjoy doing, where they met. All the things together made one **big** friendship.

The children liked the friendship bracelet so much that Miss Molly helped them make smaller ones for each other.
Kerry likes purple and so do I, so I'll use purple...
Which threads make you think about your friend?
We made friends here in this treehouse, so I need green thread.
I go swimming with my friends, so I want the blue thread next.
Here, Bim, I made this for you. Thank you for being my friend.

Miss Molly helped the class make friendship flags, to celebrate **all** the friends they had ever made. They drew pictures of them, and Miss Molly hung them on the tree, where they fluttered in the breeze.

There were friends from school, after-school friends, and even friends who were family, too. Some of the class had lots of friends and some had just one. It turned out there were **all kinds** of friends, and that was just **fine**!

Then the bell rang for the end of the school day. Miss Molly was so pleased with Kerry's class that she gave each animal a **friendship badge**, just like this one.

Everyone came down the tree to where the grown-ups were waiting.

When the Koalas got home,
there were animals playing outside.

Kerry felt a little swirl in her tummy,
but this time she knew what to do.
She put on her **biggest smile**...